FLYING FIREFIGHTERS

To the memory of Gifford Keeth
a pilot who died in a helicopter crash
while fighting a forest fire
in California in 1991

Clarion Books
a Houghton Mifflin Company imprint
215 Park Avenue South, New York, NY 10003
Text copyright © 1993 by Gary Hines
Illustrations copyright © 1993 by Anna Grossnickle Hines

Library of Congress Cataloging-in-Publication Data

Hines, Gary.
    Flying firefighters / by Gary Hines ; illustrated by Anna
Grossnickle Hines.
        p.   cm.
    Summary: Describes how a group of firefighters use a helicopter
to help put out a forest fire.
    ISBN 0-395-61197-0
    1. Forest fire fighters—Juvenile literature.   2. Aeronautics in
forest fire control—Juvenile literature.   3. Helicopters—Juvenile
literature.   [1. Forest fires—Prevention and control   2. Forest
fire fighters.   3. Aeronautics in forest fire control.]   I. Hines,
Anna Grossnickle, ill.   II.   Title.
SD421.23.H56   1993
    634.9′618—dc20   92-35500
                                                                              CIP
                                                                              AC

WOZ   10   9   8   7   6   5   4   3   2   1

Gary Hines

FLYING FIREFIGHTERS

Pictures by
Anna Grossnickle Hines

Clarion Books · New York

"Copter Five-One-Seven," the radio blares. "Reported fire in Eagle Meadow area, possible lightning strike. Please respond."

The helitack crew springs to life. The crew members put flight suits on over their firefighting clothes. Tom, the pilot, is the first to the helicopter.

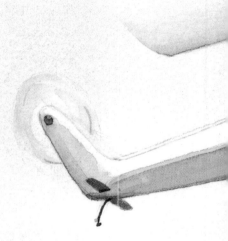

The jet engine screams awake as the rotors start
to turn. *Whop! Whop! Whop!* The giant blades
chop the air.

"Let's go!" yells Dale, the crew boss, as he and
four other firefighters jump aboard.

The helicopter floats up, and off they go!

Down below, the ridge top slides away. Almost
instantly, they are hundreds of feet above a big
canyon.

The helicopter vibrates, but seat belts hold the riders snug. Everyone looks out the windows, trying to see the smoke.

"There it is!" Joan calls out. A thin plume rises straight up. Tom sees it too and banks the helicopter sharply.

"Stanislaus, Copter Five-One-Seven!" Dale calls the forest dispatcher.

"Go ahead, Five-One-Seven."

"We're over the fire. I think we can handle it until the ground crew arrives."

The smoke cloud is growing and turning darker. The trees get closer. The helicopter settles down in a clear area and the firefighters jump out. They have to watch their heads. The rotors are still turning.

"Set up the bucket!" yells Dale. The big canvas bucket will hold water to dump on the fire. Joan and Dennis unfold it and hook it to the bottom of the helicopter. The other firefighters unload equipment.

Then the whirling craft slowly rises with the
bucket dangling beneath it.

The five firefighters remove their flight suits
and grab tools. Joan takes the portable back
pump. It's like a huge squirt gun. The others take
shovels and scraping tools.

They hike toward the fire, trying not to trip as
they hurry through the brush. Branches and twigs
slap at their bodies.

Crackle! Snap! The air fills with smoke and stings their eyes.

"I see it!" Dennis cries, pointing. The fire is burning in low brush.

Dale looks the situation over. "Scratch a line along here. We'll need a bucket drop up there to cool things down so we can work."

Sizzle! Pop!

Joan and Dennis are surrounded by thick smoke. They move away a moment to keep from getting sick.

They soon recover and go back to scraping the line down to bare dirt. Dirt doesn't burn. The line will halt the flames.

Meanwhile, Tom has flown to a lake, where he hovers and lowers the bucket into the water. As soon as it fills, he flies back to the fire.

Whoosh!

The helicopter skims over the trees. "We need a drop where the darker smoke is," Dale calls on the radio.

"I see it," Tom answers.

He circles the helicopter around. Its engine whines. The water bucket swings beneath like a rock on a string. Tom slows the ship and carefully drops in low. If the bucket catches on a tree, the helicopter could crash.

Tom pushes a release button. A snout drops down from inside the bucket. It looks like the end of a balloon hanging from the bottom. With it comes a big spray of water that hisses as it settles on the flames. Now the crew can get in closer to fight the fire.

"Beautiful drop!" radios Dale.

23

The firefighters get busy while the helicopter goes back for more water. The noisy ship returns and Dale tells Tom where to put the next drop. "On the tall tree burning below us."

The big pine has been struck by lightning. They've found the source of the fire. A white streak spirals down the tree trunk all the way to the ground where lightning peeled away the bark. The pine is burning in its top. A flying spark could land outside the scratch line and start a new fire.

Tom hovers over the burning tree. The bucket snout drops. Bull's-eye! The water drowns the sparks. The tree will still have to be cut down to insure that the fire is dead out.

More firefighters scramble up. The ground crew drove in, but had to leave their truck at the end of the road. Their leader talks to Dale.

"Looks like everything's under control here," she says. "Thanks for the help. We can handle the rest."

The helitack crew heads for the landing site
where the helicopter is waiting.

"Good work," Dale says.

They stow their gear and climb aboard, happy
to have stopped a fire before it got out of control.

The firefighters are tired, but their work isn't over until they have cleaned and sharpened their tools and put all their equipment in order. It's fire season, and they have to be ready to go again at a moment's notice. If they are lucky, they will have some time to rest before the radio blares again, "Copter Five-One-Seven. Reported Fire..."

More About Forest Fires

Many wildfires are started by natural occurrences such as lightning. A lightning fire may start right away, or it can smolder in the duff for days before flames appear. Firefighters call this a sleeper.

Other fires are started by people. A few individuals purposely light fires; others do so accidentally by leaving a campfire burning or tossing away a lighted cigarette.

The number of wildfires that occur in a given year varies considerably. It depends on burning conditions, weather, and people's carelessness. In a recent year, approximately 123,000 wildfires burned over 5,454,000 acres in the United States. More than 10,000 of those fires were on National Forest lands.

The largest fire in recent memory burned 1.4 million acres in and around Yellowstone National Park in 1988, and required the most massive firefighting effort in United States history.

A big fire usually requires hundreds, perhaps thousands, of firefighters, and several helicopters—often twenty or more. Small helicopters might make bucket drops, while larger ones are used to ferry heavy cargo. Helitack crews may stay on a big fire for weeks.

In the early days, when it seemed impossible that people could ever run out of trees, forest fires were often left to burn over vast areas. Then in the late 1800s people began to realize the earth's supply of trees and other natural resources was not unlimited, and a major campaign to put out wildfires began.

Eventually, scientific studies showed that fire was not necessarily always bad. It can provide new food for wildlife, can help an aging forest renew itself, and enables many natural processes to take place.

Today, fires started by people are always put out. Naturally caused fires, however, are sometimes allowed to burn in wilderness areas where human life and property are not in danger. People are still debating about the balance between letting natural fires take their course and protecting the forest for human use. The Forest Service and the National Park Service continue to experiment with intentionally reintroducing fire back into nature under controlled conditions.